_____

_____

This book belongs to

To Emily, Eleanor & Freya
M. C.

For William, with love, Rosi x
R. B.

First published in Great Britain in 2007 by Gullane Children's Books
This paperback edition published in 2008 by

Gullane Children's Books
an imprint of Alligator Books Ltd
Winchester House, 259-269 Old Marylebone Road, London NW1 5XJ

1 3 5 7 9 10 8 6 4 2

Text © Michael Catchpool 2007
Illustrations © Rosalind Beardshaw 2007

The right of Michael Catchpool and Rosalind Beardshaw to be identified as the author and illustrator
of this work has been asserted by them in accordance with the Copyright, Designs and Patents Act, 1988.
A CIP record for this title is available from the British Library.

ISBN: 978-1-86233-710-7

Printed and bound in China

You Won't Shift a Hippo

Michael Catchpool

Rosalind Beardshaw

GULLANE
CHILDREN'S BOOKS

It was hot and the sun shone down on
a winding river...
a wobbly bridge...
and a very sleepy hippo.

The hippo was huge,
the hippo was heavy...

and the hippo was
in the way.

'This is terrible!' said a tawny Lion. 'My favourite shady spot is on the other side of that bridge and I can't get to it with that hippo lying there. He will have to move.'

'You mark my words,' squawked a green and blue parrot who sat watching from the trees. **'You won't shift a hippo if it don't want to go!'**

'Nonsense!' said the lion.
'He'll move for me. Don't you
forget I am king of the jungle.
I will **ORDER** him off the bridge.'
And he strolled right up to
the sleepy hippo.

But the hippo didn't move . . . not one little bit.
'**Don't you realise who I am?**' roared the lion
again, shaking his impressive mane.

'*NOW MOVE!*'

But the sleepy hippo just
slept on — snoring as he did.
'See,' squawked the parrot,
'I told you so.'

'What on earth's going on?' asked a long-tailed monkey scrambling down from the trees. 'There's ripe, juicy fruit on the other side of that bridge and I can't get to it with that hippo lying there. He will just have to move.'

'But he won't! We've tried to **ORDER** him off . . . but he just won't go!'

'Then we must **PUSH** him off the bridge,' said the monkey. 'Come on.'

'But wait,' squawked the parrot. '*You won't shift a hippo if it don't want to go!*'

'**HOGWASH!**' said the monkey. 'Just you watch.' And they made their way up to the sleepy hippo.

'One, two, three, **PUSH!**'
But the hippo didn't move . . . not one little bit.
'*PUSH HARDER!*' roared the lion.
'That's all right for you to say,' puffed
the monkey. 'I've got the heavy bit here!'

But the sleepy hippo just slept on — snuffling as it did.
'See,' squawked the parrot, 'I told you so!'

'What a kerfuffle!' said a bristly warthog as he lumbered along and noticed the hippo on the bridge. 'The best mud for rolling in is on the other side of that bridge and I can't get to it with that hippo lying there. He will have to move.'

'But he won't! We've tried to **ORDER** him off, and we've even tried to **PUSH** him off . . . but he just won't go.'

'Then we must try something else,' said the Warthog.
'We must **BOUNCE** him off the bridge.'

'But stop,' squawked the parrot. '**You won't shift a—**'
'And you can help too,' snapped the lion as he grabbed the
parrot's beak. And they all made their way to the bridge.

'Ready, steady... jump!'

Up they went —
and then . . .

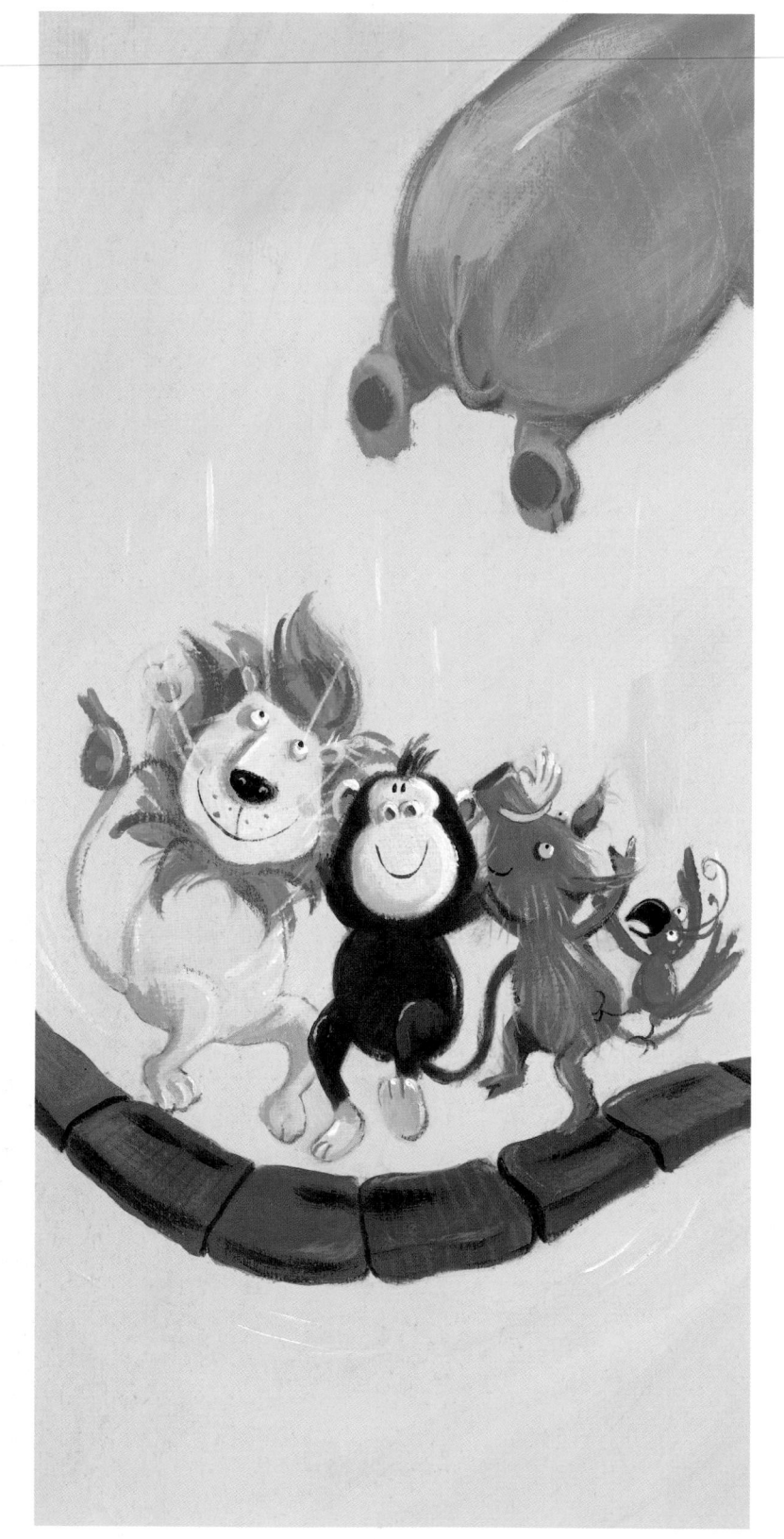

Down they went on the wobbly bridge. And as they went down, the hippo went **up**.

'Hooray!'

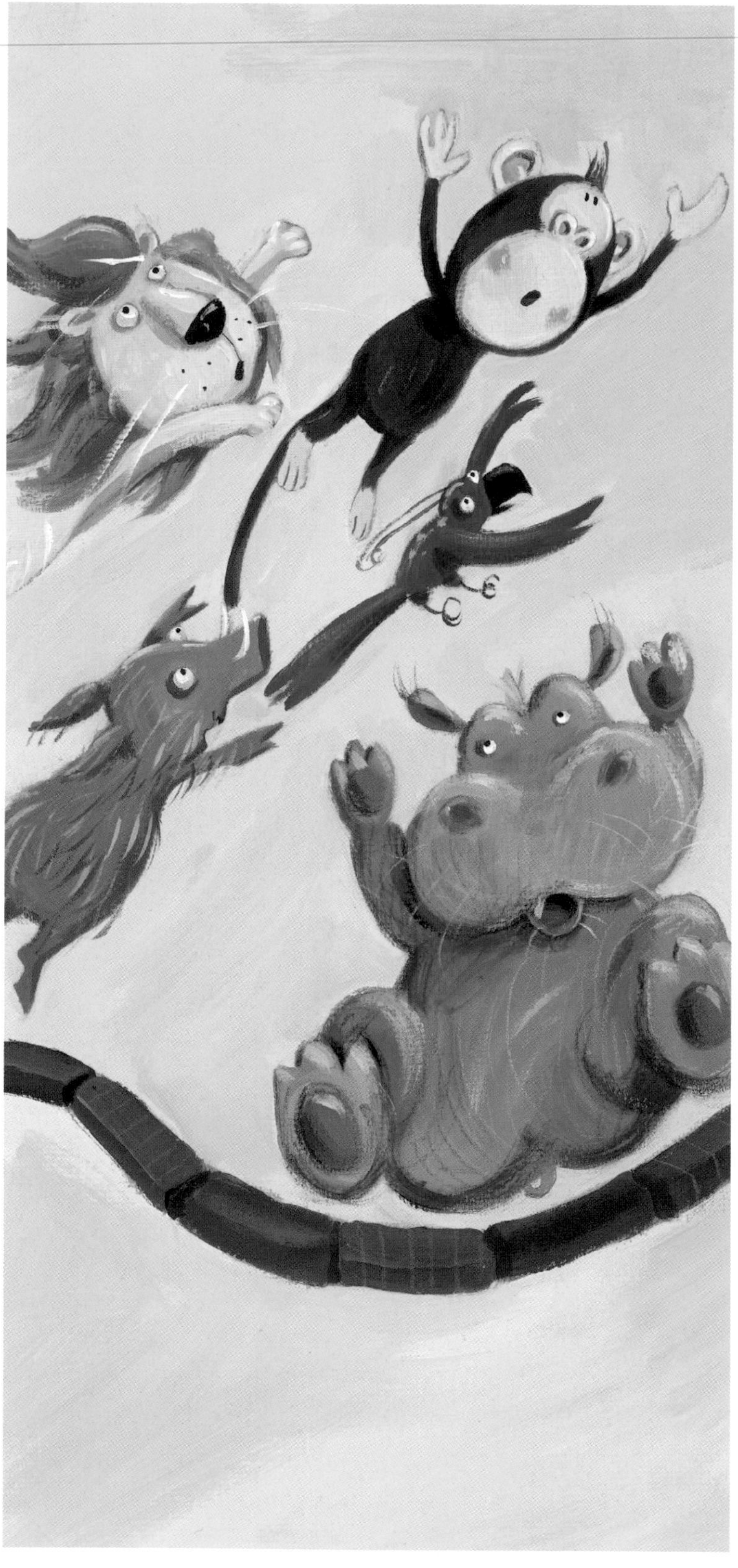

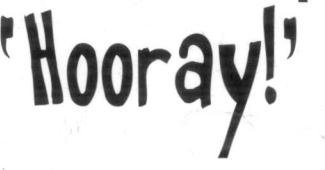

But then the hippo went **down**. And when the hippo went down the others went . . .

up... and **up**... and **up**...

And then

down...

and

down...

and

down...

...into the river below!

Splash!

'See!' squawked the parrot as he dragged himself out of the water.

'You don't need to say it!' snapped the lion.

'Excuse me,' squeaked a little mouse as he
hurried along, 'what seems to be the trouble?'
'We're trying to cross the bridge but that hippo just won't move!

We've tried to **ORDER** him off,
We've tried to *PUSH* him off,
And we've even tried to **BOUNCE** him off . . .

but he just won't go!'
'Let me have a try,' squeaked the little mouse.
And he scampered towards the sleepy hippo.

He wriggled his nose and twitched his whiskers and whispered into the hippo's ear.

And with an enormous *yawn*
the hippo stretched and got up.
And he and the mouse wandered
off across the bridge, side by side.
'Wow,' squawked the parrot as
they all stared at the huge, heavy
hippo and the tiny, little mouse.
'What ever could he have said
to make that hippo shift?'

And the little mouse
turned round and smiled.
'Please!' he said.

Other Guillane Children's Books illustrated by Rosalind Beardshaw

Snog the Frog
TONY BONNING (AUTHOR)

A Tale of Two Goats
TOM BARBER (AUTHOR)

The Lamb-a-roo
DIANA KIMPTON (AUTHOR)